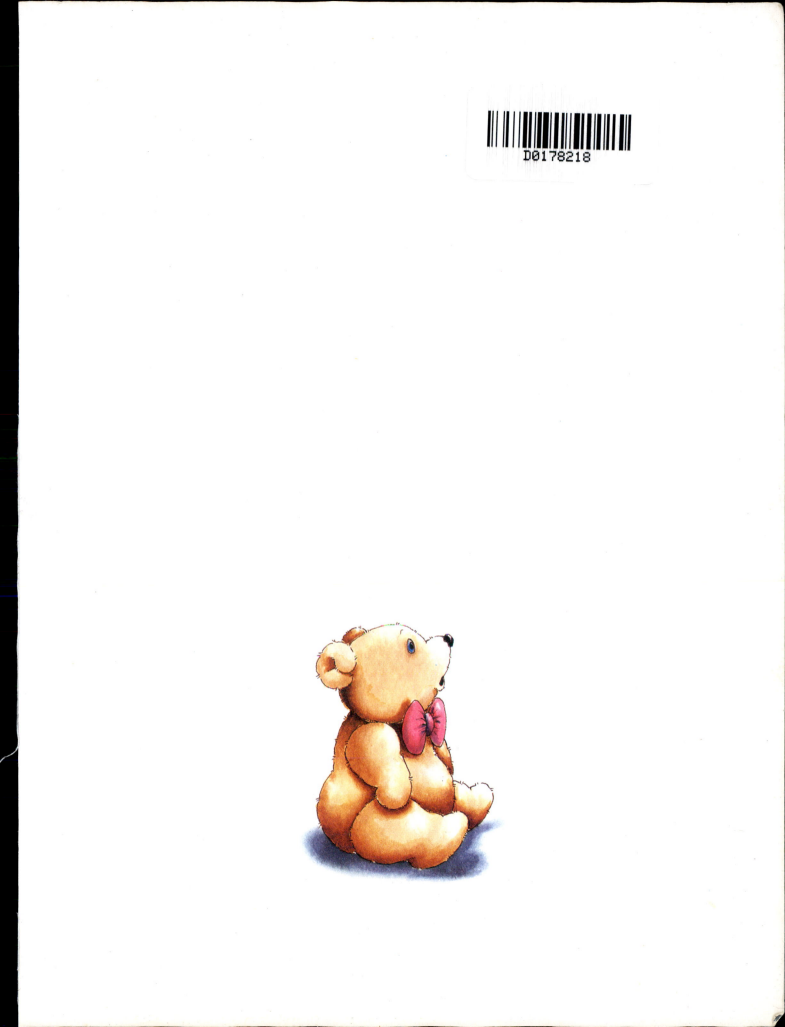

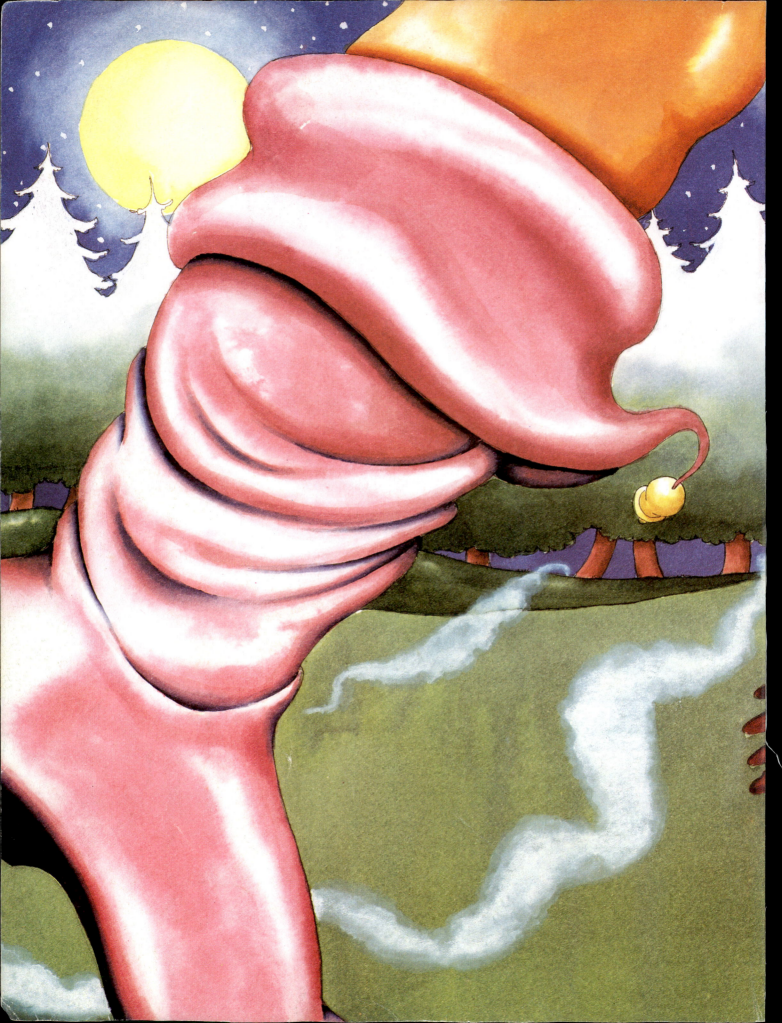

For Christy John Blance,
with love.

A catalogue record for this book is available from the British Library

Published by Ladybird Books Ltd Loughborough Leicestershire UK
Ladybird Books Ltd is a subsidiary of the Penguin Group of companies
Text © LADYBIRD BOOKS LTD MCMXCVI
Illustrations © Nigel McMullen MCMXCVI
LADYBIRD and the device of a Ladybird are trademarks of Ladybird Books Ltd

The Giant Walks

by Judith Nicholls
illustrated by Nigel McMullen

Picture
Ladybird

The giant walks,
up from the page…

over the ceiling…

down the window,
onto the floor…

along the carpet,
through the door...

out of the gate…

A midnight moon
paints the forest white…

and beneath the trees…

the giant walks…
don't talk, don't talk!

The giant creeps...

on his dream-time walk.

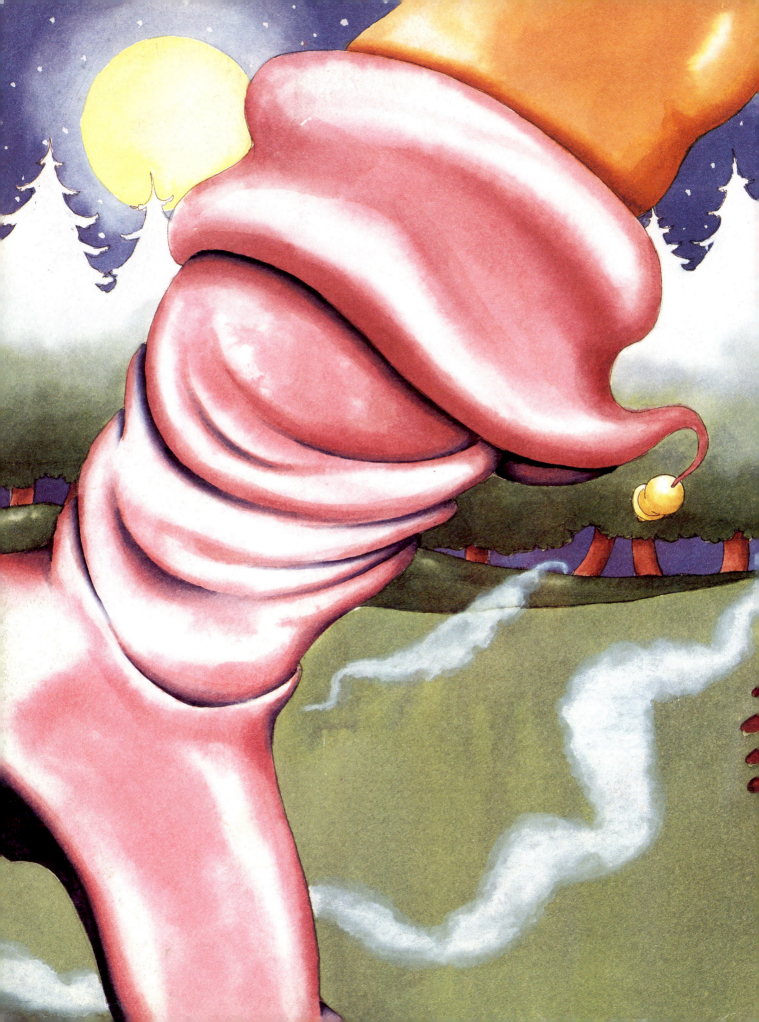

Picture Ladybird

Books for reading aloud with 2 – 6 year olds

The exciting *Picture Ladybird* series includes a wide range of animal stories, funny rhymes, and real life adventures that are perfect to read aloud and share at storytime or bedtime.

A whole library of beautiful books for you to collect

RHYMING STORIES

Easy to follow and great for joining in!

Jasper's Jungle Journey, Val Biro
Shoo Fly, Shoo! Brian Moses
Ten Tall Giraffes, Brian Moses
In Comes the Tide, Valerie King
Toot! Learns to Fly, Geraldine Taylor & Jill Harker
Who Am I? Judith Nicholls
Fly Eagle, Fly! Jan Pollard

IMAGINATIVE TALES

Mysterious and magical, or just a little shivery

The Star that Fell, Karen Hayles
Wishing Moon, Lesley Harker
Don't Worry William, Christine Morton
This Way Little Badger, Phil McMylor
The Giant Walks, Judith Nicholls
Kelly and the Mermaid, Karen King

FUNNY STORIES

Make storytime good fun!

Benedict Goes to the Beach, Chris Demarest
Bella and Gertie, Geraldine Taylor
Edward Goes Exploring, David Pace
Telephone Ted, Joan Stimson
Top Shelf Ted, Joan Stimson
Helpful Henry, Shen Roddie
What's Wrong with Bertie? Tony Bradman
Bears Can't Fly, Val Biro
Finnigan's Flap, Joan Stimson

REAL LIFE ADVENTURE

Situations to explore and discover

Joe and the Farm Goose, Geraldine Taylor & Jill Harker
Going to Playgroup, Geraldine Taylor & Jill Harker
The Great Rabbit Race, Geraldine Taylor
Pushchair Polly, Tony Bradman